The Trail of the Hunter's Horn

The Trail

of the Hunter's Horn

By BILLY C. CLARK

Illustrated by Veronica Reed

G. P. Putnam's Sons

New York

To Mom

Bertha Hewlett Clark, whose heart is as free as the water of the Big Sandy River.

To Dad

Mason Edwin Clark, whose lonesome fiddle sings as sweet as a mountain wind.

Contents

1. *Waiting for Jeptha*

Jeb stood by the window and looked down the narrow path winding like a brown snake through the willow saplings on the banks of Catlettscreek. It would be along this path, he knew, Uncle Jeptha would come, his big shoulders pushing the willow limbs out of the path. In front of him, swishing her long tail, would be his small redbone hound, Lucy. Lucy would not be bringing a pup with her this time, according to Jeptha. It would be a while longer. Today, Jeptha had said, he would come to tell Jeb how he was to earn the pup Lucy was going to find.

7

Every time the wind lifted the willow limbs along the path Jeb caught his breath and waited. He held his breath until the wind died and the willow limbs swayed back in place. Ever since Jeptha had told Jeb about earning the pup, Jeb had done little but think of how he would be asked. Maybe, he thought, Jeptha would ask for money, and there were not many ways a boy could earn money here in the Big Sandy Valley this time of year. From the signs of the sky, Grandma Quildy said the water from the creek would rise over the bank early and flood the bottoms. Ground would be broken late and there would be little work in the bottoms until late spring. By this time, Jeb would be too busy raising the garden at the cabin to work for neighbors. Jeptha would be upriver cutting the tall trees and rafting them to float down to the mouth of the Big Sandy River, and he would not be home to help with the garden. Grandma Quildy was old and could not do much work.

Jeb turned from the window and looked toward the fire grate. Grandma Quildy sat in her rocking chair reading the Bible. The flames from the fire flickered a light across the wrinkles of her face and down her long, gray hair.

"Grandma Quildy," Jeb said, "do you reckon Uncle Jeptha will sure enough come today?"

"Before dark if the Lord's willing," Grandma Quildy said, placing a pine split between the pages and closing the Book. She looked toward the window and squinted her eyes at the dark clouds hovering over the steep ridge above the cabin.

The clouds came every year at this time. And Jeptha came from the hills every year at this time. And always Jeb stood by the window and waited. Grandma Quildy would always mumble a prayer that Jeptha be guided along the tramroads to the cabin.

Jeptha was a big man and Jeb knew that he knew the hills. He had helped build most of the tramroads. And when the creek swelled early, Jeptha knew the shallow places to cross. A man as smart as Jeptha would be needing little help from a Book, Jeb thought.

There were many things Jeb did not understand about the Bible. When he was younger, Grandma Quildy had told him that this Book had guided his mother and father up the steep hill-path to the ridge to rest a while. And then the Book had sent him to live with her. This Book had placed a cover of earth over his mother and father to shield them from the snows of the winters and from the sun and rains of the summer. One day they were to be brought up from the ground and led to a home beyond the clouds, above the mountains. This Book would guide them.

Once Jeb had asked Grandma Quildy if hound-dogs lived beyond the clouds and she told him that she could not find any print in the Book that said they did. Jeb told her if they did not he didn't believe he would care to go there and she scolded him. He asked Jeptha once about it and was told that Grandma Quildy's eyes were failing with old age and she couldn't see the print in the Book too well. What she couldn't see she made up, Jeptha figured.

"How would you be able to hunt if there were no hound-dogs there?" Jeptha had said.

This had been some time ago and Jeb figured he had learned many things. But he still believed that Jeptha's knowing the signs of the hills would be all he needed to guide him home.

It was dusk when Jeptha came up the path. The black clouds had opened and emptied the rain and when Jeptha came through the door he was soaking wet. He walked to the fire and Grandma Quildy handed him a towel. She told him that she had been worried about his coming home during time of storm.

"Swam the creek with one hand and guided Lucy with the other," Jeptha said, laughing and rubbing the towel through his hair.

The door opened and Lucy stood with her nose just inside. She held her head low and turned her eyes toward Jeptha. Her tail made a thumping noise against the side of the door.

"Come in, Lucy," Jeptha said, looking toward Grandma Quildy, knowing Lucy would track water across the floor and shake more from her hair.

Lucy came farther into the room. Her hair was parted by the rain from her nose to her tail. She was the prettiest hound Jeb thought he had ever seen, even though Grandma Quildy had said Lucy's tail was too long for just one dog. Her hair was the color of the redbird, and her eyes as black as the sparrow's. Her tail was long . . . the longest Jeb had ever seen on just one dog.

Once Jeptha had told Jeb that he could have sold part of Lucy's tail. A man at the timber mill by the name of Chet Potters had asked to buy it. Chet's sister had sent him a bulldog from over in West Virginia and it had come to the hills without a sign of a tail on it. That is, nothing but a short stub.

"Now whoever heard of a dog without a tail on it here in the hills?" Jeptha had said, laughing.

Chet had been kidded so much about the tailless dog that he had offered to buy part of Lucy's, according to Jeptha. He had intended to sew part of it onto the stub of the bulldog's.

"Now whoever heard of a redtailed bulldog here in

the hills?" Jeptha had asked. "Worse yet, whoever heard of a bobtailed hound?"

It didn't seem possible, but Jeb had seen his Uncle Jeptha graft limbs to trees and make them grow and he was not sure. If it were true, then he was glad that Jeptha had not sold part of Lucy's tail. A bobtailed hound would look funny, he thought. And a good hound could well be judged by the swish of its tail. This he had heard from Jeptha, and Jeptha knew all there was to know about hound-dogs.

Jeb sat at the table waiting for Jeptha to eat. He was not hungry himself yet he knew he must wait until his Uncle Jeptha had finished before he could ask about the pup. Hound-dog talk had no place at an eating-table, according to Grandma Quildy. But when Jeptha filled his plate again Jeb became restless and said:

"I want to ask you something, Uncle Jeptha."

"Not at the table, Jeb," Grandma Quildy said.

Jeptha finished the plate and pushed it into the center of the table.

"Reckon we'll have to go into the other room to talk," he said.

Jeb followed Jeptha in by the fire grate and when Jeptha sat down in the rocking chair, Jeb squatted on the floor. Jeptha filled his pipe and slid a match over the arm of the chair. He looked toward the other room for Grandma Quildy. He knew if he had been seen striking the match on the arm of the chair he would be scolded.

"I reckon," he said, blowing out a white puff of smoke, "what you want to ask is concerning this pup Lucy is about to find."

"Reckon," Jeb said, scooting closer to the chair.

"Been doing some thinking about this pup," Jeptha said. "It ought to be a powerful pup." Jeptha wrinkled his face and rubbed his chin. "Hound-pup is worth a heap of money here in the hills. A man from the hills has got to have a hound-dog. They all can't have one like Lucy, and I figure this pup to be about as close to her as you can get. Some of the men at the timber mill have asked me a price already. Chet Potters has bid highest so far."

"Maybe he is after the tail," Jeb said, still wondering if it were possible to graft the tail onto the stub of a bulldog.

"Maybe," Jeptha said. "It's not my concern to ask what he wants the pup for; it's the money he will pay. Once sold, the pup is his."

Jeb looked at Lucy. She was curled close to the fire.

"Grandma Quildy says the creek will rise early this year," Jeb said. "I won't be able to work along the bottoms to earn money. But I am willing to work. I could go back to the hills with you and work until I made enough money to buy the pup."

"Can't do that," Jeptha said. "Got to be someone here to look after Ma and take care of things."

Jeb looked toward the kitchen where Grandma Quildy was washing dishes. He was thinking that if he had to stay home to work, then by rights Grandma Quildy should help him talk for the pup. But then, he thought, she had not been concerned about his getting the pup. Whenever he tried to talk to her about it, she would say that hound-dogs were men talk.

Jeb looked toward the fire, toward where Lucy lay. He knew he could not bid with Chet Potters in money. If he could not work for it then there was little hope of his ever getting the pup.

"There might be a way, though," Jeptha said. "Money is good to have, but it is not the only thing. Good, hard work goes a long way with me." Jeptha filled his pipe again and slid another match across the chair-arm. This time he did not look up, as if not concerned about what Grandma Quildy would say. "By the time I come again the creek will be swollen over the bottoms. Carp will be swimming upcreek, and you know how I like to take a spell at catching a mess. Bait is the only thing that slows me down."

"I could get the bait," Jeb said. "Lots of it." Jeb was thinking this might be the way Jeptha had decided for him to earn the pup. "I could get red worms. I know where they live." Jeb was thinking of the rich dirt beside the barn, kept warm and soft by the bedding hay he put there during the winter.

"Not worms," Jeptha said. "Worms will not be carp bait. When water covers the bottoms, worms are brought to the top, out of the ground, and the carp get all they want. They get independent when it comes to worms. But . . . say a man was to have some doodlebugs. That would be real carp bait."

Jeb thought of the doodlebugs. They were small, white worms similar to a grubworm in many ways. Their home was underground, and there was only one way they could be caught. With a straw. Like the crawdad, they dug into the ground and left an opening. Once you had found a hole you poked a straw into it and twisted the straw around carefully. If the doodlebug was there he would move the straw and try to push it out of his hole. If you pulled gently on the straw you could draw him to the top and grab him. If you twisted too hard you would push the straw through the tender skin of the doodlebug and kill it.

But the ground had to be warmed by the sun before the doodlebug would stir, and it was early in the year.

The sun was still slow breaking through the leafless oaks on top of the ridge.

"How many doodlebugs?" Jeb said, thinking of the few he had caught last year.

"Maybe twelve," Jeptha said. "Not many doodle-bugs for Lucy's pup."

"That's a lot of doodlebugs," Jeb said, "with the ground still thawing."

"The pup will be a lot of hound too," Jeptha said. "Of course it might be too much work for you. Bids are in at the mill. I figure Chet to stay high. Maybe it's the tail, and maybe not."

Jeb thought of the twelve doodlebugs he would have to catch. And then he thought of the hound-pup walking around at the timber mill to be laughed at because its tail was gone.

"I can catch the doodlebugs," he said.

"Think about it tonight," Jeptha said. "If at daylight, when I leave, you still believe it is not too much work to catch them, you can have a chance to earn the pup."

At daylight Jeb was more determined than ever to catch the doodlebugs. Grandma Quildy looked toward the spotted sycamore that stood at the edge of the yard. Jeb knew she was judging the wind by the sway of the naked limbs. And by judging the wind she could know how soon the rain would come. Jeptha looked toward the sycamore and then toward Grandma Quildy.

"I will be at the mill ahead of the rain," he said.

Jeb walked as far as the willow grove with Jeptha, talking about the pup all the way.

"I'm depending on you, Jeb," Jeptha said, "to watch after Grandma Quildy. She is getting old and you will have to do most of the work. These doodlebugs will have to be on your own time."

Jeb stood until Jeptha and Lucy were out of sight and then he turned toward the cabin. Grandma Quildy sat in the rocking chair reading the Bible.

"A dozen doodlebugs are not very many, are they, Grandma Quildy?" Jeb said.

"Poor doodlebugs," Grandma Quildy said. "Taken from the ground to be skinned on a hook."

Jeb didn't think Grandma Quildy wanted to talk about the doodlebugs and so he walked to the creek to gather driftwood. He sat most of the day under the willows listening to the creek water. The sun was disappearing from the slopes and the birds had begun to chatter. Jeb wondered if the birds chattered because the sound of the water over the rocks kept them awake. They flew from limb to limb, as restless as the wind.

Once Jeb had thought if he listened long enough he would be able to know what the birds were saying. But now that he had grown older he knew that he never would. Nor would he ever understand the talk of the water. Jeptha did not know yet, and he knew all the signs and sounds of the hills. Jeb knew that there were many things about the dark hills that he would never learn.

The sound of the water running over the rocks, Jeb thought, was the prettiest of all the sounds of the hills. It was even prettier than the hum of the wind through the trees and it would put you to sleep if you listened long enough. Sometimes the water was loud, and sometimes so low that Jeb had to bend his ear close to hear it. But it was always there. And it was company to Jeb. Sometimes it was lonely at the cabin with just Grandma Quildy.

Sometimes Jeb caught himself mumbling back at the water. And now he was saying "poor doodlebugs," thinking of what Grandma Quildy had said. As if it were wrong to take them from the ground, according to the Book. He knew he could talk free here at the creek and the words would not be repeated.

A week passed before the rainy weather broke. The clouds disappeared and the sun began to sift early through the oaks and shellbark hickory of the ridge.

But it had been a cold winter and the ground was frozen deep. It would take a lot of sun to draw the coldness from the ground. The black loam along the creek would be the first to warm; it would take the sun longer to break through the clay on the hillside.

But Jeb knew that he would not be able to doodle for the doodlebugs in the black loam because of the rising water. The thawing of the frozen ground and the heavy rains had already begun to push the creek over the bottoms. His chance for the doodlebugs would have to come from the hillside. The garden patch would be his only chance. Made soft by the plow of last year, it would not be as hard as the clay never before turned.

So Jeb began to work the hillside above the cabin, clearing the ground. And while he grubbed the ground of sawbriars, crabgrass, and wild honeysuckle he looked for doodlebug holes. When he found a hole he lay his grubbing hoe aside and squatted to the ground, holding his straw. Slowly he twisted and moved the straw. But the only movement came from the slow wind moving down the ridge, weaving the straw back and forth. The holes that he found were smooth and level on top and he knew that these were old holes and that the doodlebugs had left them with the coming of the snows of last winter. A new hole would have a fresh mound of dirt around it where the doodlebug had shoved it out in digging the hole. But there would be little time and he knew that he must try every hole if he was to catch twelve before Jeptha came.

A week passed before Jeb spotted the first fresh hole. It had been dug close to the roots of a tall black oak that stood at the edge of the garden patch. Jeb stretched on his stomach and eased a straw into the hole. He twisted slowly and waited. The wind moved the straw and Jeb jumped. For a minute he was mad. And he took a deep breath. He knew that he was too anxious and had been fooled by the wind.

The next time he cupped one hand in back of the straw to shield it from the wind, twisted the straw and waited. The straw moved. Jeb eased the straw toward the top of the ground. He could feel the weight of the doodlebug and his heart beat fast. He spotted the head of the doodlebug above the hole and moved his hand fast to cup it. The doodlebug let go of the straw and slid back into the hole. Jeb had grabbed too fast, not letting the doodlebug come out far enough. Now the doodlebug would be wise and harder to fool. But Jeb knew he had to have him.

He eased the straw into the hole again, twisted and waited. But it did not move. He twisted again and waited. Again there was no movement. Maybe, Jeb thought, the end of the straw had split and could not reach the bottom of the hole. He was sure that the doodlebug would be at the very bottom. He pulled the straw out and looked at the end. The end of the straw was feathered and it was wet. Jeb felt the straw and wrinkled his forehead. He had been too anxious. The straw had been pushed through the tender skin of the doodlebug and now it could never be brought out. He thought of the doodlebug lying dead at the bottom of the hole, picked up the grubbing hoe and moved it slowly over the tough pods of crabgrass. It seemed as though he would never catch the doodlebugs.

The next day Jeb's hopes were higher; he spotted another fresh hole. This time he moved slowly and brought the doodlebug out. He fumbled it in his hand and looked at it for a long time. It was like holding a piece of money, and Jeb thought it had been harder to earn.

When evening came he took the doodlebug home, put it in a box of black dirt and sneaked it into his room, hiding it under the eaves of the roof. And when darkness came he lay awake and listened to the sparrows chatter outside the eaves. He could not sleep. He thought there was a chance the sparrows knew the doodlebug was in the box and that when he was asleep they would find a way into the eaves and get it.

Jeb found the next doodlebug hole under a pod of crabgrass. He had started to grub the crabgrass away when he spotted the fresh mound of dirt. He lifted the blades of grass and eased in the straw. And up came the doodlebug. Before the sun set below the oaks Jeb had caught four. This gave him five. There would be seven more to go.

In three days Jeb would have to turn the ground to plant seed, and there would be no doodling holes left to spot; only the long, red furrows. Away from the garden patch the ground would still be hard, not loosed by plow, and there would still be some coldness under the hard crust. There were not likely to be new holes in that kind of earth. But Jeb could not shun his work, because Jeptha had said the doodling must come on his own time. Grandma Quildy was depending on the garden and so the seed had to be planted in time.

Jeb sneaked the four doodlebugs to the box in his room. And he went to bed early. Tomorrow he would have to have keen eyes and watch closer than ever for new holes.

2. Lucy Caught the Moon

At daylight Jeb stood along the slope of the hill and watched the sun sift through the limbs of the oak. He bent over the hoe, scanning the ground closely, until his back ached. When he came to a large pod of grass or honeysuckle he stopped and lifted the leaves aside searching for a hole. At the end of the day he had found one. And from this hole he coaxed a doodlebug almost too small to cover a hook. He put the doodlebug in his hand, covered it with dirt and walked toward the cabin. Before he was off the slope he could see Grandma Quildy standing in the yard, looking toward him.

23

"Jeb," she said, "I'm ashamed of you, putting doodlebugs in your room. The house is no place for
worms. Something just told me to look close to the
eaves when I cleaned the room."

"But Grandma Quildy," Jeb said, "the doodlebugs
are in a box and they can't climb out. Doodlebugs
can't climb like fishing worms."

"The house is no place for them," she said. "And
you will have to take them out. I'm not going to touch
a box of worms."

"Where can I put them?" Jeb said. "I got to watch
them. Uncle Jeptha will be here any day now and I
don't have time to catch more."

"You don't have to watch a box of doodlebugs,"
Grandma Quildy said. "I never heard of a person
stealing doodlebugs. Either out they go or the chickens
get them. I won't sleep another night in there with
the thought of worms crawling around."

Jeb took the box of doodlebugs from his room and
walked into the yard. He looked for a safe place to
hide them. If he put them very far from the house he
wouldn't be able to watch them. And if he kept them
too close, Grandma Quildy was apt to feed them to
the chickens. He looked toward the woodpile under
the big sycamore. He could see this woodpile from the
window of his room. This seemed to him to be the

only place. During the day he could take the doodle-bugs to the slope with him, and during the nights when the moon was bright he could watch them from the window. On dark nights he would have to take a chance.

Jeb made a flat place on the woodpile and placed the box. He laid a flat board over the box to shield the doodlebugs from rain that might come without warning. And while he placed the box, Grandma Quildy's rooster scratched in the dirt below the woodpile, turning its head sideways and watching Jeb. Jeb threw a stick at it and it ran around to the other side of the house.

"You get my doodlebugs," Jeb said, "and Uncle Jeptha will be stringing chicken on a hook when he comes."

When night came Jeb could not sleep. The moon was gone and cold winds crawled down the high slopes and shook the limbs of the sycamore. Jeb looked from the window but he could not see the box. He thought about Grandma Quildy saying something had told her the doodlebugs were in his room. He wondered if it could have been something she had seen in the print of the Book. He wondered if the Book had the great powers she often spoke of. Uncle Jeptha *had* always made it from the hills, and at times the weather had been bad. There was a chance the prayers Grand-ma Quildy said for him had something to do with guiding him.

If Jeb lost the doodlebugs, he lost the pup. If there was any chance at all in the power of the Book it was worth a try. So Jeb knelt beside his bed.

"Lord," he said, "I don't rightly know if it was You who told about the doodlebugs being in my room or not. And I wouldn't be caring if there was a moon tonight and I could see to the woodpile. You must know, I reckon, that they are out there. Grandma Quildy says You know everything. What I'm wanting to ask is that You help me watch the doodlebugs until Uncle Jeptha comes. I can watch them myself during the day, and if You can sorta keep an eye on them at nights for me I'd be obliged. In case You don't know everything like Grandma Quildy says, I want to tell You that I think the danger is in that rooster of Grand-ma Quildy's. He knows the doodlebugs are there. No matter how hard I try I can't see the woodpile tonight. Amen."

Jeb was at the woodpile when daylight broke. In front, lying on the ground, was the box. The black dirt was scattered over the red clay of the yard and the doodlebugs were gone. There were chicken tracks in the dirt. Jeb looked around the yard. The big rooster flapped its wings beside the house. Jeb grabbed a stick and ran after him. The rooster squawked and Grandma Quildy came out of the house.

"What are you doing to that rooster, Jeb?" Grandma Quildy said.

"He got my doodlebugs!" Jeb said. "He watched me put them on the woodpile and waited until I was asleep. You knew all the time if I was to put them there the rooster would get them. You never wanted me to have the pup!"

"Lord help me if I knew the rooster would get the doodlebugs," Grandma Quildy said, wringing her hands.

"Lord didn't help me last night when I asked Him to help me," Jeb said.

"The good Lord had nothing to do with the doodlebugs, Jeb," she said.

"He had nothing to do with guiding Uncle Jeptha home, either," Jeb said. "I asked Him to help me and He helped the rooster. It was a high climb to the woodpile and the rooster couldn't have made it himself without a light to see. Chickens are blind in the dark."

"You have no faith, Jeb" Grandma Quildy said, wiping her forehead with her apron. "If you had had, perhaps you wouldn't have needed the doodlebugs in the first place. You pretended to have faith last night, but you can't fool the Lord."

"And I don't have time to fool twelve doodlebugs," Jeb said. "How will I ever get the pup?"

"Maybe it is not too late for faith," Grandma Quildy said. "But you would have to believe with all your heart. Last night you prayed for the Lord to watch the doodlebugs and then you got up in the night and went to the woodpile to see about them. I heard you. You didn't have faith that the Lord could watch them."

"I'll never get the pup," Jeb said.

"I will search the print," Grandma Quildy said. "You search for faith. Strange things are written in that Book."

On the weekend Jeptha came. Jeb was on the hill and it was not until he came down and saw Lucy that he knew Jeptha was there. He ran to the house.

"Did you bring the pup?" Jeb said, catching his breath.

"Bring me the doodlebugs," Jeptha said, in a slow voice.

Jeb looked toward Grandma Quildy and she lowered her head.

"I reckon," Jeb said, "there is something I ought to tell you about them doodlebugs."

"Don't have to," Jeptha said. "Just bring them to me so I can count them."

"I don't have the doodlebugs," Jeb said. "Grandma Quildy's rooster went to the woodpile where I was hiding them and ate them."

It was hard for Jeb not to cry. Yet he didn't want Jeptha to see the tears. Tears were not the mark of a man, or of a boy the size of Jeb. But he had worked hard and had not shunned his work. The doodlebugs had been caught. Grandma Quildy just sat with her eyes lowered. There was nothing Jeb had to offer for the pup. Nothing except maybe this faith that Grandma Quildy had spoken of. And this seemed very small compared to the box of doodlebugs. Yet it was the only chance.

"Grandma Quildy said," he said, "that faith could be counted same as the doodlebugs."

"Perhaps . . ." Jeptha said. "Perhaps that's what it was."

Jeb looked down at Jeptha and then toward Grandma Quildy. Grandma Quildy had raised her eyes and looked toward Jeptha.

"Coming through the hills this morning I had the funniest feeling," Jeptha said. "As if something was calling my name. I thought it was the wind through the trees. You know how the wind will sometimes catch in the knothole of a tree and make a sound that you can reason to be a voice. But Lucy began to whimper and she hung her long tail between her hind legs and crouched close to me. I tried to make out the sound and for some reason I got to thinking of the doodlebugs. I thought of the work that had been left here to do while I was away at the mill.

"Surely, I figured, this feeling is only from the sound of the wind, and so I looked up into the tall hickories where this sound seemed to be coming from. I found a knothole in the tallest tree and waited for the wind to catch it again. It did. But somehow it didn't sound like the wind. I've never been as keen on this faith as I ought to be, but I have sense enough to know I've been guided along the tramroads for years without asking. Maybe if I had started earlier the trips would have been shorter and I wouldn't have had to lean on Ma's faith all this time. Faith is a better bait than a doodlebug, Jeb, and I reckon the pup is yours."

Jeb's heart beat so loudly that he was sure it could be heard across the room. Grandma Quildy laughed and wiped her eyes. And Jeptha walked to the other room and came back holding the small, red pup. He handed it to Jeb.

Jeb looked at the pup. The pup had one eye as black as the sparrow's; the other eye was as white as the bark of the sycamore. Jeb looked at the broad head and long ears. And then he looked at the tail.

"Look!" he said, pointing to the stub. "Uncle Jeptha has sold the pup's tail!"

"Wait a minute," Jeptha said. "How can you sell a tail when there was no tail to sell?"

"There was a tail," Jeb said. "All hound-dogs have tails. There is a part of it left. Its eyes are not even the same color. They both ought to be as black as the sparrow's, like Lucy's."

"Don't you know what that white eye is, Jeb?" Jeptha said. "That's the mark of the moon. You don't find it in a thousand dogs."

Jeptha slid a match over the arm of the chair and Grandma Quildy scolded him.

"I learned it years ago," Jeptha said, "from an old hunter that lived as close to the mountains as the black oak. Do you know why it is, he said, a hound-dog howls from the ridge at night when it is not treed? And why it will set all night and bark at the moon, first on the flat, then up the slope, and then from the highest peak? Not many men would know the dog is chasing the moon; the dog is trying to find a pup. They know the moon is the sign of the night and if they can catch it the moon will mark the pup with the signs. Not many dogs catch it. Most of the hounds

give up and settle for an ordinary pup. Lucy didn't quit, Jeb. She trailed night after night. And that bulldog of Chet Potter's went with her. Sometimes I would catch a glimpse of her along the steep ridge and hear her deep voice along the slopes. She must have climbed the tallest mountain and sunk her teeth in the moon.

"Now, I figure that Lucy pulled the moon close enough to the peak for the bulldog to grab ahold. The moon marked her pup with the signs of the night; a mooneye, the old hunter called it.

"Now as for the tail, it was in all rights that the moon give the bulldog something if he sunk his teeth in. And I figure it was the stubtail, like the one he had. A mooneyed hound is one in a thousand."

"Maybe we could graft a tail on the pup," Jeb said.

"The pup will be stronger with the stub," Jeptha said. "The fewer limbs a tree has, the more powerful the trunk. It ought to work the same on a hound-dog. That's going to be a powerful pup."

"Grandma Quildy," Jeb said, "I think you have good eyes to see the print in the Book with."

"What made you think my eyes were bad, Jeb?" Grandma Quildy said.

"If I was you, Jeb," Jeptha said, "I believe I'd take the pup to bed. It is small and will need lots of rest for the trails it will run."

"Come on, Mooneye," Jeb said, picking up the small pup in his arms. Lucy followed behind, whimpering and wagging her long tail.

Jeb tucked the covers over the pup and placed its head on the bed beside his. Lucy curled up at the foot. The pup whimpered.

There was no need for the pup to be afraid, Jeb thought as he rubbed the pup's hair. What it heard was only the wind in the sycamore. Jeb looked toward the sycamore. Then he looked up the steep slope, toward the ridge. Way above the ridge he could see the moon.

But Jeb could not sleep. During the night the wind became stronger and the pup began to whine. Lucy kept moving from the foot of the bed to look at the pup. Each time Jeb scolded her and she went back to the foot of the bed. Each time he had to wait until she circled around and around before lying down. Lucy always circled before lying down and Jeb thought of the night on the dark ridge that Uncle Jeptha had told him the reason.

Dogs had learned this from the foxes and wolves, according to Jeptha. They circled so that if a hound struck their trail while they slept, and got close, they could move on. And the hound would circle and circle when he came to their bedding place, trying to work out the trail. This would give the fox or wolf time to place distance between them.

The wolf was no longer on the mountains, but Jeb had watched foxes circle and lie down. But he didn't see why Lucy had to circle and keep him awake. There was nothing after her. (419275

It seemed to Jeb that he had just fallen asleep when Lucy sprang from the bed and woke him. And in the dim light he could see her cross the floor, wagging her long tail. The pup tried to follow and Jeb held it with one hand and rubbed his eyes with the other. He squinted and looked toward the door.

He could see the tall shadow of Jeptha standing in the doorway. He patted Lucy and walked toward the bed. Jeb could see that he carried something in his hand.

"Are you awake, Jeb?" he said.

"Yes," Jeb said, sitting up straighter, still rubbing his eyes.

"The wind is high in the trees," Jeptha said. "I am going to go early to beat the rain. I brought you something to keep while I am away."

He held out his hand.

36

Jeb rubbed his eyes again to be sure that the little light from the gray rain clouds was not fooling his sight. He could hardly believe what he saw. But there it was. A horn. A hunter's horn.

"If you are going to train the pup," Jeptha said, "he must be trained to the horn."

Jeb reached and took the horn. He raised it to his lips and blew as hard as he could. He didn't worry about waking Grandma Quildy if she was still asleep. He was too happy.

But the horn didn't blow. "I can't blow it," he said, trying again and again. "Neither can the pup follow a trail yet," Jeptha said. "The horn can be blown only by a hunter. But you are like the pup, Jeb. You have not followed many trails, so you will have to train like the pup. And when you are able to blow the horn, the pup will have learned to trail."

Jeptha spoke to Lucy and turned toward the door. Lucy stopped when she heard the pup whine and Jeptha spoke to her again. She whimpered back at the pup and then turned, stopping at the edge of the door. Jeb could see Lucy, her head low, looking back at the pup. She wagged her long tail and turned out the door.

Jeb gripped the horn tight. He let his fingers run over the smooth horn and up the rawhide that was tied to both ends so that the horn could be slung across the

shoulder. He thought of the sweet music of the horn,
music that was inside it. It was a sound that he hadn't
forgotten since the first time he had heard Jeptha use
it to call Lucy from the trail. Never before had Jeptha
offered to let Jeb blow the horn. Jeptha had always
kept the horn as close to him as Lucy.

And now Jeb could hardly believe that he held the
horn in his own hands.

"The horn can be blown only by a hunter" — Jeb
kept thinking these words that Jeptha had said. And
he wondered how long it would be until he would blow
the music of the horn through the tall trees over the
ridges and into the deep valleys. He could see himself
standing on the slopes with the horn to his lips. And
he could imagine Mooneye fighting his way through
the heavy underbrush, coming in to the sound.

A hound always comes to the sound of a horn —
that is, a good hound. A horn is the only thing that
will break a good hound from a trail, even if he is in
sight of the game. Only the horn. And once trained
to the horn, the voice cannot call him in.

Lucy was a hound, and one blast of the horn made
her turn. And so might Mooneye, Jeb thought. He
was Lucy's pup. He was a hound, and according to
Jeptha, one hound in a thousand. Not even Lucy had
a mooneye and she was the best in the Kentucky hills.

Jeb was so happy about the horn that he had forgotten to walk to the willows with Jeptha. He looked
through the window, now, but there was not enough
light to see down the path. He laid the horn beside him
and pulled up the covers. The horn was nearly as big
as the pup. Jeb watched the pup curl into the curve of
the horn and lie still.

3. The Bobtailed Hound

The early spring rains pushed the young sprouts of corn out of the ground and Jeb knew that he would have to go every day to the hillside garden and grub out the tough crabgrass that grew between the hills of corn. Once the crabgrass got a start it would grow so fast that it would soon choke the young corn. It would leave nothing but dried corn-hills under the hot sun that had come to the mountains.

Each morning with his hunter's horn hung across his shoulder and the small pup jumping at his feet, he put the grubbing hoe over his shoulder and left the cabin.

"Sure don't look like a workingman going to the hills to me," Grandma Quildy would say. "Looks sure enough like a hunter." Then she would look at the pup. "Remember the crabgrass, Jeb. It grows most as fast as that pup."

And Jeb thought Grandma Quildy was right. For every time he noticed the pup it seemed to get bigger. Everything about him was growing. That is, all but the stubtail. His ears hung almost as low to the ground as Lucy's. His body was small, but like the corn, Jeb thought, it too would grow fast with the summer. Only the mooneye and stubtail kept him from being the prettiest hound Jeb thought he had ever seen, including Lucy. And every time Jeb looked at the tail he thought of what Jeptha had said about the less limbs a tree had, the stronger the trunk.

At first, Jeb thought he'd name the pup Stubtail. Now he was glad he hadn't. Once he had named the pup he would not have been able to change the name. It was bad luck to change the name of a person, according to Grandma Quildy, and Jeb thought it might be the same with a hound-dog. There was a good chance he might get used to the stubtail. Already he did not notice it as he had at first.

There was one thing Jeb had set his mind to. He would keep Mooneye in the hills until he had been trained to be the best hound in Kentucky and then no one would be able to laugh, stubtail or no stubtail. Jeb didn't believe anyone would laugh at the mooneye. If they knew anything about hunting they would be sure to know that it was the mark of the moon. And they would know that Mooneye was one dog in a thousand. And this to Jeb seemed like an awful lot of dogs. Jeptha himself had said this and he knew more about hound-dogs than anyone else. The only laugh might come from the stubtail.

While Jeb weeded the corn the small pup ran up and down the rows sniffing at the ground, and sometimes he would stop to dig after the field mice. And there were times he would run over the small corn and Jeb would have to scold him.

At first, Jeb had kept the horn across his shoulder. But toward the end of the day under the hot sun the horn became heavy and it bounced against his side as he moved the grubbing hoe forward. He took the horn off and hung it on a low limb of the black oak near the edge of the garden where he had caught his first doodlebug. And when he hung the horn across the limb he thought of the doodlebug. He thought of all the work he had done only to find that he hadn't needed the doodlebugs in the first place. Grandma Quildy must have found words in the Bible that said he was to get the pup. All he had been asked to do was to search for faith. And Jeb had not searched, actually. Enough of it seemed to come without searching too hard. He had not told Grandma Quildy that he had not really ever believed the Book could get him the pup. Perhaps, he thought, he had fooled Grandma Quildy. And maybe the Book, too. But he had the pup now, and there was really never any need to tell. He would keep it a secret.

Jeb grubbed the crabgrass away from the corn and pulled it into the center of the rows. Here the grass, with roots torn from the ground, would wilt under the hot sun and most of it would be blown away by the wind. He pulled the soft dirt up around the corn so that it could hold more water when the rain came. There would be many days, he knew, when there would be no new rain, only what was held in the ground.

Each time he circled the field he stopped at the oak and raised the horn to his lips. Each time he took a deep breath and blew with all his might. But still there was no sound. While he tried to blow the horn, Mooneye would turn his head sideways and look up at Jeb and the horn as if he were trying to understand what they were both trying to do. When the sound of air came from the end of the horn the small pup

would jump up and down in front of Jeb as if he wanted to play. Sometimes Jeb thought Mooneye was making fun because there was no music coming out of the horn.

"You ain't supposed to watch me while I practice," Jeb would say. "You ought to be out in the brush training yourself. Then one day when I blow the horn you will be able to follow a trail as well as Lucy."

The pup would whimper and run a short distance down the rows of corn and then he would turn and come back to stare again at the horn. Jeb would place the horn on the low limb and work out another row of corn. And each evening he slung the horn across his shoulder and walked to the cabin.

"I didn't hear the horn today, Jeb," sometimes Grandma Quildy would say. "You must have been too busy working to stop and try."

And Jeb would think of the many times during the day he had stopped under the shade of the oak and touched the horn to his lips. There were even times that he thought the horn was not a true hunter's horn and it would never blow. But he had watched Jeptha blow the horn too many times to know that this was not true.

"Maybe the horn won't blow," he once said to Grandma Quildy.

"The music is in the horn, Jeb," she said. "Just you keep trying and one day you will hear more than the wind."

"Did it say in the print of the Book that I might be able to blow the horn?" Jeb said, remembering how easy it had been to get the pup without the doodle-bugs. If there had been power enough in the Book, Jeb was thinking, to get the pup for him then surely there was enough to let him blow the horn.

"The Book speaks of a horn, Jeb," Grandma Quildy said. "It tells of a man by the name of Gabriel who has been trying to blow the horn longer than the mountains have stood. One day he will blow the horn. And all the good people will walk up the mountain slopes toward the sound of his horn and on into the clouds. Gabriel has faith, and one day he will blow his horn. Now you ain't been practicing near that long, Jeb."

Jeb didn't know how old the mountains were but he knew that they had been standing for a long time. Deep gullies, cut by rain water running from the hills, marked the mountainside. They were like the wrinkles of an old person's face. Jeb looked at the wrinkled mountain and then at the wrinkles in Grandma Quildy's face. They were both old, Jeb thought, but the mountains were much older.

"I hope I don't have to wait that long," Jeb said.

"Maybe you wouldn't if you had enough faith," Grandma Quildy said, turning away.

Jeb worked the corn until it grew so tall that he could no longer see his horn if it hung from the low limb of the oak. And so as the corn grew he hung the horn to higher limbs so that he could see it from anywhere in the field. When the corn became too tall for him to see the horn he stretched the rawhide back over his shoulder and carried the horn with him through the field.

He kept the horn with him all the time and almost everywhere he went, the horn went, too. And with him went the small pup. There was only one place the pup could not follow Jeb. And that was when Jeb went to the store down the creek and across the ridge to the edge of town. Once a week Jeb went to get supplies for Grandma Quildy. Each time he walked down the path the pup tried to follow. Jeb would have to scold him and the pup would stop in the middle of the path and lower his head, never letting his eyes leave Jeb.

Most of the time he waited on the path until Jeb was out of sight and then he would try to follow. And Jeb would have to turn and run him back to the cabin. When he came from the store the pup was always lying in the middle of the path, down from the cabin, waiting. And when he saw Jeb he would run down the path to meet him.

Once Grandma Quildy had scolded Jeb for leaving the pup behind.

"You ought to be ashamed, Jeb," she said, "leaving the pup to whimper and watch the path until you get back."

"But it doesn't take as long by myself," Jeb said.

"You carry the horn," Grandma Quildy said, "to catch on the brush. A horn is no good without a hound. If you are prouder of the horn than the pup then you don't deserve the pup. It is no fault of the pup's that his tail is stubbed and one eye is . . ." Grandma Quildy took the coal oil that Jeb had gone for and turned away.

Jeb walked to the creek and sat under the willows thinking of what Grandma 'Quildy had said. He watched the small, white blooms of the willows glide with the wind and fall into the smooth water of the creek. Once on the water the wind would push the white blooms to the edge of the bank and then they would drift with the slow current downstream. Jeb heard Mooneye whine and he watched him slow-trailing the tracks of a muskrat. Jeb could see where the muskrat left the mark of his tail on the soft mud at the bottom of the creek.

Even the muskrat had a long tail, Jeb thought. The trail led to a hole in the mudbank. The entrance to the hole was under water. But Jeb knew that the hole turned back up into the bank where it was dry. The entrance was under water so that the muskrat could be safe. Out of the hole stuck a piece of cornblade, drifting back and forth with the current of the creek.

Jeb thought of the trouble he could save the pup if he could tell him about the muskrat the way Jeptha had once told him. But tracking the muskrat would be good practice for the pup. The short stub of the pup moved back and forth. At the edge of the water he stopped. He sniffed the top of the water and whined. Jeb called him and he came back and sniffed the horn lying across Jeb's lap.

Maybe it was wrong, Jeb thought, not taking Moon-eye with him to the store. But still Jeb knew there would be men at the store. There always were. And he was afraid they might laugh. He didn't want anyone to laugh at the small pup. This was not being ashamed, he thought, like Grandma Quildy said. One day the pup would learn to follow the trail, and Jeb would learn to blow the horn. There would be no reason to laugh then. He would show them by the music of the horn and by the game that he would catch.

4. The Mark of the Moon

Ever since Grandma Quildy had scolded Jeb about leaving the pup at the cabin he began to dread the days he must go to the store. Before, it had been a comfort to Jeb. But before he had been able to take his time along the trail. He could stop often and listen to the signs and sounds of the woods. But he had told Grandma Quildy that without the pup he could make a fast trip and now he had no time to stop.

Jeb was sitting up on the hill watching the tassels of the corn blow in the wind when he heard Grandma Quildy calling for him. The week had passed fast and already it was time for him to go for supplies. The horn was lying at his feet and the small pup was digging in the soft dirt to find a cool bed below the hot outer crust of ground standing open to the sun. Mooneye heard Grandma Quildy as soon as Jeb did and he stopped digging and looked down the slope toward the cabin. He wagged his short tail, threw his head into the air and ran a short distance down the path. Then, he stopped and waited for Jeb. Jeb picked up the horn, slung the strap across his shoulder and started down the slope. Mooneye ran ahead to the bottom of the path and turned once again. He waited there for Jeb.

"Have you forgotten that today is the day to go to the store?" Grandma Quildy said. "We are out of coal oil again, and from the sign of the sky, darkness will come early tonight. Hurry, now, or we might be sitting in the dark."

Jeb had not forgotten about going to the store. He had thought about it all morning. He thought again about leaving the pup. Maybe, he thought, Grandma Quildy would tell Jeptha about it when he came. And Jeptha might take the pup from him. Somehow he didn't think Grandma Quildy would ever understand. It was not, Jeb thought, that he didn't care for the pup. He would never want to give the pup back to Jeptha.

Grandma Quildy would never understand that Mooneye was probably the only stubtailed hound in the
mountains. Jeptha had said himself that he had never
heard of a stubtailed hound. And he had laughed.
Jeptha, Jeb figured, had seen more hound-dogs than
anyone. Jeb knew that he would have to wait some
more before taking the pup to the store.

He followed Grandma Quildy into the cabin and
waited for the money that would buy the coal oil.
Grandma Quildy handed him an empty jug.

"Be careful of the coal oil, Jeb," she said. "It is not
hard to spill."

Jeb looked at Mooneye. And then he took his hand
and lifted the hunter's horn from his shoulder and
laid it across the mantle.

"Aren't you going to take the horn?" Grandma
Quildy said, looking surprised.

"The horn is kinda heavy," Jeb said. "And it slows
me down some. Sometimes it catches on the bushes."

Jeb did not look at Grandma Quildy when he spoke.

"The store is no place to take a horn," he said.

"Leave it if you like," Grandma Quildy said. "But
don't go so fast that you spill the oil."

At the edge of the willow path Jeb stopped and
looked back. Mooneye stood in the center of the path
looking toward him.

"You will have to wait with the horn," Jeb said, motioning toward the cabin with his hand.

Mooneye lowered his head and turned toward the cabin. Jeb started down the path.

The path followed the course of the creek for almost a mile and as Jeb walked he listened to the sound of the water. There was no wind in the valley and the limbs of the willows hung low to the ground.

At the forks of the creek the path turned and crossed the ridge. Jeb stopped and took one last look up the path toward the cabin. Then he turned up the path with the jug swinging in his hand. Out of the willows he stepped and under the beeches that grew the lowest on the ridge. Jeb heard a noise in one of the beeches and he stoppped. Along one of the limbs a redbird pecked at a green beechnut. Jeb watched the small redbird peck and then turn its head sideways as if it expected to hear something. As he watched the redbird he thought of the red hair of the pup. In a way he wished he had brought the pup with him. He could see Mooneye, lying in the path, his eyes turned down-creek watching every movement of the low hanging willow limbs. Jeb knew that with any movement the pup would jump, thinking that Jeb was coming out

of the willows. But the store was not too far away and Jeb thought he would be home soon.

On up the path the trail became steeper. Jeb stopped beside one of the large gray rocks and looked back over the valley. He looked over the tops of the beeches he had come through. They were close together and seemed to grow in circles around the mountainside. The leaves were white, and against the green that had come to the valley with the early sun, the tops of the white beeches looked like winding trails of smoke.

Beside the rock where Jeb stood grew the green rock moss. The moss was as green as a young blade of corn and as soft as the pink and white bloom of the wild honeysuckle. To the left and right of the rock, and on up the steep path, grew the tough black oak, sprinkled with a few shellbark hickories. Jeb thought as he looked toward the oaks that it would take a tree this tough to stand against the strong winds of the ridge. The higher on the ridge the less limbs the oaks seemed to have, and the shorter they became. The trunks were rounder and their bark was so thick and tough that the claws of the squirrel would not mark it. Jeb looked at the oaks, and again he thought of the small pup. He thought of the short tail and what Jeptha had said about the tree with fewer limbs having the most strength. And according to Jeptha it ought to be the same with a hound-dog. Jeb hoped so. He knew the power of the short-butted oak. Where many hillside gardens had been cleared for the plow a short-butted oak had been left to stand to be circled by the plow, too powerful to be pulled from the ground by a team of mules.

When Jeb reached the top of the ridge he thought he heard something in the underbrush. He leaned against one of the black oaks and listened. There was a light wind in the trees, but there was almost always a light wind on top the ridge. Today it was not strong enough to fool a person with the sounds it could make through the trees.

Jeb heard the noise again, and looking to the left side of the ridge he caught a glimpse of something red slipping through the thick underbrush. And then it disappeared. Jeb slipped farther behind the black oak and waited. He peeped around the side of the tree. Once again he saw the brush move and caught a glimpse of red.

Jeb took a deep breath. It was a fox, he thought. Only a fox could move as quietly in brush that had not been dampened by rain for several days. It was a red fox, Jeb thought.

Jeb waited a while longer; longer than he knew he should. He had told Grandma Quildy that by leaving the horn and the pup he could make a fast trip. He had stopped to look at the redbird in the beeches. He had stopped to look at the tops of the beeches and the green rock moss, and he stayed too long under the black oak and shellbark hickory. And now he was wasting time trying to see a red fox.

Jeb picked up the jug and started out the ridge. The ridge tapered until it came to a point, and at the point Jeb turned down a path that led again into the valley. A short distance from the foot of the path would be the store.

Jeb had gone halfway down the mountain when he heard something again in the underbrush. He stopped and looked back up the path. The sun had passed over his head and was shining at an angle against the black oaks, throwing a shadow of the trees across the path. The red-clay path with the shadows of the oaks across it looked like a long ladder that Jeb thought he could use to climb back up the mountain once he had the oil.

Jeb held his breath and listened. He could hear the steps of something walking on the dried leaves in the underbrush. But the brush grew so thick that he couldn't see through it. The leaves that rattled on the ground were the leaves of last year, Jeb knew. The brush was so thick now that a fresh leaf could not fall

through it. If a leaf fell from a tree it would have to lie on top of the brush until the brush died. Then, and only then, could it reach the ground.

It could be, Jeb thought, that the fox he had seen on the ridge was traveling the same way he was going. On the low slopes ground had been turned for corn and it would be here that the field mice lived. And there was nothing a fox would rather do than dig in the soft dirt for field mice. There was no wind here on the slope and Jeb knew that his scent could not be carried to the fox. Or then maybe, Jeb thought, the fox was smart and figured it could outrun him. There had been a time or two when he was squirrel hunting and a fox, after an all-night run from the hounds, had come within a few feet of him. It circled and lay down to rest and wait until the hounds worked the trail closer.

Jeb picked up a rock and threw it into the underbrush. He heard the run of soft feet for a short distance and then the mountainside was quiet. He picked up the jug and headed down the path.

At the foot of the slope he stopped and looked toward the store. He knew he would have to hurry now and not waste time getting back over the mountain. He walked a short distance and looked overhead toward the sun. When he had left, the sun had been almost to the top of the mountain. Along the ridge, while he had waited to watch the fox, the sun had been over his head. And now it had started down the other side of the mountain.

He lowered his eyes from the sun and glanced again toward the mountain path. And once again he saw something red. Jeb caught his breath.

Out of the trees walked Mooneye. He came a few more feet and then stopped, watching every move Jeb made.

Jeb knew that the red he had seen on the mountain had not been a fox. Mooneye had followed him all the way from the cabin, keeping to the underbrush so he could not be seen. He knew that it had been wrong for him to follow and so he had hidden. And Jeb was mad.

"Mooneye!" he yelled.

The small pup ran down the path and jumped up and down in front of Jeb.

"You knew it was wrong for you to sneak and follow me!" Jeb said.

Mooneye stood at Jeb's feet and whined, looking Jeb straight in the eye. His red hair was covered with cockleburs and was full of red dust where he had crawled along the mountaintop to keep from being seen.

"You stay here!" Jeb said, in a coarse voice, "until

I come out of the store. And then you wait until I get you home."

The pup whimpered and crawled closer to Jeb's feet. Jeb's eyes softened and for a minute he wanted to speak soft words and pat him on the head. It had been a long trip fighting the underbrush. But it had been wrong for Mooneye to follow when he had been told to stay at the cabin. Lucy would have stayed if Jeptha had told her. She was trained to mind. But then Jeb knew that Jeptha would never tell Lucy to stay behind on just a trip to the store. But Mooneye was different, Jeb thought. A young pup could get lost in the hills.

Mooneye lay on the path, his head across his paws and his eyes fixed on Jeb. Jeb watched the short tail push away the dirt, wagging back and forth. Once again Jeb thought of the words he had not been able to forget since the day Jeptha had said them:

"Whoever heard of a bobtailed hound here in the mountains?"

"Stay here!" Jeb said. And he turned toward the store. He stopped at the door and looked back. Mooneye still lay on the path, watching.

"Come for more oil, Jeb?" Mr. Tate said, walking from behind the counter. He wore a white feedsack apron and moved slowly. He was smiling at Jeb. But he was always smiling, and this was one of the reasons Jeb liked him so well. And he would sometimes talk to Jeb if no one was in the store. He would tell him tales of the woods and tales of the great hounds he had known. When he first saw Jeb with the horn he talked about it. He knew it belonged to Jeptha. And he told Jeb that Lucy was the greatest hound he had ever seen. He had sat many nights on the store steps and listened to her sing to a coon on the ridge. Then toward daylight he heard the sound of the horn.

Jeptha had stopped at the store on his last visit and told Mr. Tate about the pup. And now everytime Jeb came, Mr. Tate asked about the pup and asked Jeb to fetch it some trip.

"Horn getting too heavy, Jeb?" he said, as Jeb handed him the jug.

At the end of the room on a wooden chair sat Bunt Borders, a foxhunter. And on another chair sat a man that Jeb didn't know. The strange man whittled at a stick and looked up once when Jeb walked in. Then, he started whittling again.

Mr. Tate walked over to a steel drum and opened a spigot at the end. He placed the neck of the jug over the spigot and looked at Jeb.

"Didn't bring the pup this trip, huh?" he said.

Jeb caught his breath quickly. He turned and looked

back up the path. Mooneye was no longer lying there.

"Lucy's pup," Mr. Tate said. "Sure would like to see it."

"Coonhound or foxhound?" the strange man said, not looking up.

"Being Lucy's," Mr. Tate said, "it would have to be a coonhound. And anything like her and it would be the best."

Jeb swelled his chest and for a minute he felt proud of the pup.

"Just like Lucy," he said.

"Red fur and all, I'll bet," Mr. Tate said. "Long ears, long tail and all, huh?"

Mr. Tate held the jug out to Jeb but Jeb didn't take it. He looked toward the door. In the doorway stood Mooneye. He looked at Jeb with his head low and wagged the stubtail.

"'Pon my honor," Bunt Borders said, looking up. "A bobtailed hound." His laugh sent cold chills over Jeb.

"He's a coonhound," Jeb said. The pup heard Jeb's voice and it came to him.

"Part coonhound, you mean," Bunt Borders said. "All of him ain't there. Never thought I'd see the day. All that bragging Jeptha has put up. Look here, Sill."

The man that had been whittling looked up.

"First one I ever saw in the mountains," he said, laughing. "Got a white eye, too."

Jeb's eyes became watery and he looked toward Mr. Tate. There was no smile on Mr. Tate's face and he looked at the two men with a frown.

"It's sure enough Lucy's pup," he said. "Pretty as a redbird. Long ears, long . . . sure enough Lucy's pup."

Bunt Borders stooped beside the pup and moved his hand back and forth of the pup's head on the side that had the white eye. The pup trembled at Jeb's feet.

"That's the mark of the moon," Jeb said, wondering if Bunt Borders would know that it was a mark on one in a thousand dogs.

"Don't know much about hounds, do you, boy?" Bunt Borders said. "Don't you know, and ain't Jeptha ever told you, a mooneyed dog is blind in the white eye?"

Tears streamed down Jeb's face. He looked toward Mr. Tate. Mr. Tate squinted his eyes. He looked again at Bunt Borders and then back at Jeb. He patted Jeb on the shoulder.

"I reckon he's right, Jeb," he said. "But . . ."

Jeb grabbed the jug and ran from the store.

Jeb was halfway up the mountain slope before his wind gave out and he had to stop to rest. He sat down under a shellbarked hickory and wiped tears from his eyes. The small pup lay at his feet, panting from the climb up the mountain. Its eyes did not leave Jeb and when Jeb sobbed it whined and crawled closer to him.

The sun had started down the side of the mountain and the wind was heavier in the trees. The woods were full of sounds and the tops of the black oaks swayed under the wind. Jeb looked at the black oaks and they seemed to lose their strength. Even the short-butted oaks swayed under the wind. And to Jeb they seemed as weak as the sumac.

Jed didn't notice the beeches at the top of the ridge. He didn't stop to look at the moss. If the redbird was still in the beeches, Jeb didn't see it. Behind him trailed the small pup, stopping now and then to sniff the ground and then running to catch up. Jeb turned under the willows and hurried up the path toward the cabin.

He walked straight in the door and handed Grandma Quildy the jug of oil. She felt the oil on the outside of the jug and then raised it to the light from the fire grate.

"You've been running, Jeb," she said. "You might have spilled all the oil on your way home."

And then she looked at Jeb and saw the redness of his eyes.

"You've been crying, Jeb," she said. "Did the pup follow you?"

"Grandma Quildy," Jeb said. And then he stopped. He could not say what he wanted to say. His eyes welled with tears and he pointed toward the white eye of the pup that was standing inside the door. "My pup is blind. You and Jeptha knew it all the time."

5. Sampson on the Mountain

Jeb did not take the horn with him to the garden. It had lain on the mantle since the first day he had put it there. Most of the times the small pup went with him but Jeb paid little attention to it. And before long the pup seemed to sense that something was wrong and sometimes he would leave the field without Jeb and go down the path to the cabin. But he was always standing at the foot of the path when Jeb came home in the evening.

Grandma Quildy did not speak much to Jeb about the pup. She began to take the pup into her care. Many evenings now she was the one who fed it. She let it have all the rights of the cabin, and it went in and out as it pleased. Sometimes it lay at her feet while she read from the Bible.

One evening she caught Jeb staring at the horn and she said:

"The music is still in the horn, Jeb."

Jeb didn't answer. He took his eyes from the horn and he was determined that Grandma Quildy would never catch him staring at it again.

Each morning he went to the hillside garden. The tassels had turned brown on the corn and the ears were full enough to pull from the stock. Leaves had begun to turn brown on the trees and the blades of corn touched the ground. Sometimes during the day Jeb would stop to watch a flock of wild geese flying over. And he began to spot wild ducks in the creek. These were all sure signs of winter; it would be in the mountains soon. From the signs of the sky, Grandma Quildy said it would be early this year. Jeb knew that the hair on the coon and possum was turning to a winter coat. They would be out to feed at nights now. The coon would be in the cornfields and on the creek hunting crawdads. The possum might be anywhere.

Jeb watched the brown leaves glide from the black oak at the edge of the garden. They glided through the air like small brown birds, and then struck a gust of wind and turned end over end to the ground. The sound of the wind through the trees reminded Jeb of the hunter's horn and he thought of the weird sound of the horn drifting through the trees on the mountainside. There were times that he wanted to run down the path to the cabin and grab the horn and run into the yard and blow with all his might. But the horn was no good without a hound to trail. The music of the horn would only drift along the mountain slopes and die in the valleys.

Frost came early to the hills, and at night the fog lifted from the creek and settled over the low ground. The tall oaks on the ridge looked still and bare. Sometimes at night Jeb would look up the steep ridge and he could see the moon in the clear sky. But the moon was no longer pretty to Jeb. Instead it seemed to mock the white eye of the pup.

And now there was little time that Jeb had for the pup. Winter brought more work for him at the cabin. There was corn to cut and shock during the day and driftwood to gather at the creek. And Jeb wanted to gather enough driftwood to last the winter before the snows fell.

One evening when Jeb came up the path with an armload of driftwood he saw Grandma Quildy standing in the yard looking toward him. The pup was standing beside her and when it saw Jeb it ran to meet him.

"Come in the cabin and set a spell, Jeb," she said. "I want to talk to you."

Jeb laid the wood on the woodpile under the sycamore and walked to the cabin. Grandma Quildy sat down in the rocking chair and Jeb squatted on the floor.

"The Book speaks of a blind man, Jeb," she said. "His name was Sampson. And Sampson was the strongest man in the world. And he had more faith than a thousand men. He was so strong that he could lift a short-butted black oak out of the ground, roots and all, with one hand. And then one day, Jeb, he only *acted* as if he had faith. He thought he could fool the Lord." Grandma Quildy wiped her forehead with her apron. "Some people were jealous of Sampson's strength, just like there are people here that are jealous of a good coondog. The Lord took away Sampson's great strength, and when his enemies found it out they fought him and put out his eyes. Both eyes, Jeb. And they left him to wander along the mountain, blind. Everybody shunned him and he was left without a friend.'"

Jeb looked at the wrinkles in Grandma Quildy's face. But she did not look toward him. She looked into the fire. Mooneye lay at her feet with his head over his paws and his eyes on Jeb.

"And when Sampson was blind he remembered that he had tried to fool the Lord. And in the darkness he searched again for faith. And while he was walking in the darkness, Jeb, he found it. Maybe he heard Gabriel trying to blow the horn and followed the sound on a trail that led him back to the Lord. And the Lord looked down on Sampson and he saw his blind eyes. And beyond the eyes he saw the heart. And in Sampson's heart he could see the faith. And he gave Sampson back more strength than he had ever had. Strength enough to lift one of the mountains into the air and put it down on another. All he needed was faith."

When darkness came Jeb couldn't sleep. He tumbled in the bed and listened to the wind in the sycamore. He couldn't forget what Grandma Quildy had told him. When he closed his eyes he could see the strong Sampson wandering through the dark hills, staggering into the trees and falling and tripping over the thick underbrush, feeling his way through the darkness. His eyes looked white to Jeb; as white as the eye of the pup. Jeb felt sorry for this Sampson and he felt a lump in his throat. He thought if he had been there he would have led Sampson through the woods and shown him the way.

Jeb opened his eyes and then closed them again. This time he would see Sampson tall and strong on the mountainside. He could see his great arms as broad as the trunk of a tree lifting one of the high mountains and setting it on top of another. And Jeb felt happy that Sampson was strong again. Now he wouldn't need to be led.

And then Jeb thought of the pup. He remembered how he wished he could have led Sampson through

the woods and yet he wasn't willing to walk with the pup because it was blind in one eye. He thought of Sampson having no friends, and he thought again of the pup. He thought how he had shunned it, and how it had turned to Grandma Quildy.

There was the horn that he couldn't blow. Without the horn the pup couldn't trail to it. Sampson had faith and he could lift a mountain. And Jeb couldn't even blow a hunter's horn.

6. Jeptha Visits the Cabin

When Jeb went to cut the corn he took the pup with him. But he left the horn on the mantle. When he looked at the pup he didn't think of hunting in the tall timbers; in a way he was leading the pup like he had thought of wanting to lead Sampson. He didn't want the pup to be without a friend because it was blind in one eye. He knew how lonely the mountains could be. He knew how lonely it was for him at times when he stood by himself on the mountainside.

Jeb had not forgotten the sweet music of the horn. He heard it in every swish of the wind. But there was

73

no need to practice now, he thought. He would take care of the pup, and one day when he owned a hound like Lucy he would learn to blow the horn.

At times Jeb thought that he might be blamed for the blind eye of the pup. Jeb knew he had pretended to have faith. He had fooled Grandma Quildy into believing that he had faith enough in the Book to get the pup. Jeb knew now that he had not fooled the Book. And maybe for his half faith he had been given only part of a hound.

The pup had begun to trail. And Jeb noticed that he was good at working trails and scanning brush piles. Once he chased a rabbit and Jeb called him off. Even if he would never make a coondog, Jeb would not have him running rabbits. A coondog would not sniff more than once at a rabbit track.

One evening when Jeb came down the path the pup barked and ran toward the cabin. Jeb heard another hound bark from the cabin and he knew it was the voice of Lucy. He caught his breath. Uncle Jeptha is here, he thought. He didn't know what Grandma Quildy had told Jeptha. But Jeb felt sure she would tell him about the blind eye of the pup.

When Jeb reached the yard Lucy ran to meet him. The pup followed her, jumping up and down like it wanted to play. By now the pup was almost as big as

Lucy and, except for the stubtail and white eye, was marked exactly like her.

Jeb looked toward the cabin. He knew that Jeptha would be waiting. He thought of the day when Jeptha had told him the white eye of the pup was the mark of the moon. And he had found out from a foxhunter that the pup was blind in that eye. Before, he had thought that Jeptha had known all there was to know about hound-dogs and now he wasn't sure. Jeb took a deep breath and walked into the cabin.

Jeptha sat by the fire smoking his pipe. He didn't turn when Jeb walked in.

"See you left the horn, Jeb," he said. "Learned how to blow it already? The pup must be learning faster than I thought."

"No," Jeb said.

"Saw the pup coming down the slope," Jeptha said. "Most as big as Lucy. Looks like Lucy."

Jeptha turned and looked at Jeb for the first time. Tears filled Jeb's eyes and he turned his head. Jeptha wrinkled his face and looked toward the fire.

"Jeb," Jeptha said, "sometimes the wind will blow the top of a tree and trick a man into thinking that it is a squirrel that makes the sound. This way the wind is bad. And then, sometimes the wind will lift the thick branches of a tree aside and let you see a gray

tail of a squirrel so you can get a shot. This way the wind is good. Man's voice is the same way. Sometimes good and sometimes bad. But still you have to listen to both winds."

Jeb rubbed his eyes.

"I have been doing some thinking, Jeb," Jeptha said. "Maybe I ought to take the pup back to the mill with me. It's time the pup ought to be trained. I won't have much time but I can let it run with Lucy and she'll teach it the woods. Besides, it has got to be trained to the horn and no one here can blow it. I'll be leaving in a short while."

"No," Jeb said.

"What's this?" Jeptha said. "Maybe you ain't wanting me to take the pup. What good is a pup with a stubtail and a white eye? The old hunter that told me about the mooneye could have been blowing to the wind. But I got faith in thinking he wasn't. I know this pup will hunt. And after Lucy is gone he will be all that's left to keep her voice from dying from the mountains. The pup means a lot to me. With me it will be wanted."

"But I want the pup," Jeb said.

"What about the mooneye?" Jeptha said. "And what about the horn?"

"I have tried to blow the horn," Jeb said. "But there is nothing in it but the wind."

For the first time Jeptha smiled.

"Takes a hunter to blow the horn, Jeb," he said. "Takes a man that has faith in the dog he is blowing to. You got to be close to your dog; close as the leaf to the tree. When you are, the music will come from the horn."

"Then I'll learn to blow the horn," Jeb said.

"Maybe you will at that," Jeptha said. "When I

leave I'll be taking the rafts downriver. Lucy can't go this trip and so I'll leave her here with you. Take her with you to the hills. Let the pup run with her and she'll teach it the trail. But remember, Jeb, only you can teach it the horn."

When Jeptha left, Jeb took the horn from the mantle and walked as far as the willow grove. At the willows Jeptha stopped.

"The old hunter wasn't blowing to the wind, Jeb," he said. "Your pup carries the mark of the moon. You will have to believe this."

Jeptha turned down the path and Lucy followed. Jeptha turned and pointed his finger back toward Jeb.

"You will stay this time, Lucy," he said.

Lucy wagged her long tail and whimpered. She stood watching Jeptha walk down the path. But Jeb knew she wouldn't follow.

7. A Hunter's Horn

Jeb could tell by the warmness of the wind that it
would be a warm and clear night. So clear and warm
that Grandma Quildy feared rain. And when Jeb took
the hunter's horn and strapped it across his shoulder
and picked up the flashlight she cautioned him for the
second time.

"Hunt low on the slopes tonight, Jeb," she said. "If
it rains you won't have far to get to the cabin. I am
afraid of the woods during time of storm. Don't stay
out too late. Circle the slopes one time and then come
in."

Jeb was so anxious to go that he didn't answer
Grandma Quildy. He was happy to have a hound like
Lucy to hunt with, and on such a clear night there
was a good chance he might strike a coon. He did not
like to have Grandma Quildy warn him about the
woods. He knew the woods well enough to name all
of the trees, and almost all the sounds.

But Grandma Quildy knew the woods as well as he
and this was why she had told him to hunt the slopes.
She knew the danger of the woods during a storm.
The tall trees on the ridge would be the first to catch
lightning if it were to strike close to the mountain.
During a storm there was always a high wind and
trees were cracked and thrown across the path. During a storm was the time when the trees shed their
dead or weak limbs, and one could hit you without
warning.

Jeb walked to the outhouse and got an empty feedsack and tucked it in his belt. Lucy whimpered and
sniffed around the yard anxious to get started, and
the small pup ran after her trying to play. But Lucy
would have no part of the pup. Once in the woods she
would hunt the trail, her own trails, and it was up to
the pup to keep her pace.

Grandma Quildy stood by the window and Jeb
waved at her and started down the path. He followed

the creek to where the path turned up the ridge and here he stopped. Lucy went into the beech grove and Jeb waited for her to circle. The pup followed her. Jeb knew that he would wait for Lucy to hunt a section of the ground. If she struck no trails she would come in. This would be a sign to Jeb to move along.

To the left of the path stood a gray rock, and in front of the rock ran a small creek. Under the rock was a good place for coon or possum. If a coon was denned under the rock, Jeb figured he was probably out of his den by now running the small creek searching for crawdads. The coon would probably work up the creek toward the head of the hollow. On the ridge there was a cornfield — a good place for coon.

While Jeb waited for the dogs to circle he walked over to the rock and flashed his light under it. He could see by her prints in the dust that Lucy had been here ahead of him. And beside Lucy's tracks were the tracks of the pup.

There were several holes under the rock and Jeb knew that each hole was a den. He dropped to his knees and reached his hand back in one of the holes. He picked up a handful of dirt and, holding it under the light, let it sift through his hand. Mixed in the dirt were long gray and white hairs. This is the den of a possum, Jeb thought.

The second and third hole belonged to a possum, but the fourth belonged to a skunk. The hair from this hole was black and white and coarser than the possum's.

None of the holes were worn slick, and Jeb figured they were old holes. And he had not really expected to find coon hair here anyway. He knew that a coon took to a tree den more often than a rock den.

The beeches near Jeb were likely to be chosen by a coon. Few beeches grew old and tall without having coon holes in them. And in these holes the coon would stay. Jeb shone his light into the tall beeches. There were several holes.

At some of the beeches Jeb stopped and shone his light on the bark. If a coon climbed the tree often, the bark of the beech would tell on him so. There would be claw marks on the slick, gray bark. Jeb found some marks on the beeches but they were mostly squirrel marks.

Lucy came back down the creek, the pup still with her. She sniffed again at the holes under the rock and started back up the creek. Jeb pulled the rawhide strap of the horn farther up on his shoulder and walked toward the head of the hollow.

Jeb didn't stop until he got to the top of the ridge. There he sat down on a dead log that had fallen across the path on his side of the cornfield, and waited for Lucy and the pup. In a short while Lucy came up the path behind him and he hissed her and the pup into the cornfield. Under the light of the moon he could follow them with his eyes to the edge of the cornfield. Behind Lucy, with its nose to the ground, went the small pup. Lucy stopped, sniffed, and then disappeared.

It seemed to Jeb that he had been sitting on the log a long time. Lucy had stayed out longer than usual. Jeb sat and listened to the wind in the trees. Now and then a bird fluttered from a tree into the darkness and each time Jeb jumped, thinking that Lucy was coming in. But each time when Lucy did not come he knew that the bird had probably been pushed from the limb by another bird and would have to find a new roost.

Jeb listened to the weird sounds of the woods. There was the hoot of an owl from over in the hollow. And from somewhere along the creek came the sound of a whippoorwill. Jeb liked to listen to the whippoorwill. Its voice was soft and clear. But not the owl. The hoot of the owl brought a loneliness to the woods.

A gust of wind swept across the ridge and Jeb listened to the sound in the trees. And then the wind died and the woods were quiet. Almost too quiet, Jeb thought.

Once, he wished that the pup would come in so that he'd have company. He had not thought it would stay out this long. But it would be wrong to call the pup in. And he couldn't call Lucy even if he wanted to. She would only come to the sound of the horn if she were out tracking.

The wind became harder in the trees and still Lucy did not come. Jeb got up to stretch his legs and walked to the edge of the cornfield. The moon was overhead and was so bright that Jeb didn't have to use the flashlight to see the path. Lucy had been gone too long, he thought. He let his hand slide along the smooth horn and he touched the mouthpiece. Then he let his hand fall to his side.

Then, in the stillness of the woods, Jeb heard it. It was Lucy's voice. Loud and clear it sounded through the woods and bounced against the sides of the valleys. Jeb jumped with joy and listened. Lucy bawled again and again, each time from a different place. They were short, quick bawls and Jeb knew she was trailing. Whatever she had struck was not far away.

Jeb waited to hear the voice of the pup. But there was only Lucy's voice. The pup is a silent trailer, Jeb thought. And he frowned. Jeb liked to listen to a hound that opened on the trail, first with short, quick barks and then a steady bawl when it had treed the game. To him this was the prettiest of all music. A silent trailer would only bark after it had treed, and some would not bark then.

Jeb listened to Lucy as she trailed the side of the slope and crossed a ridge into another hollow. She came out of the hollow and down a ridge. If she trailed over this ridge, Jeb knew, she would be in Hurricane Hollow. Hurricane Hollow was a short hollow. At the head of it stood a large rock cliff. If Lucy could turn the game into this hollow and press it close enough, she could run it into the rock. Here it would have to turn and make its stand. If it was a fighting animal, like a coon, it would make a stand and fight.

Lucy's voice stopped. Then after a short while Jeb heard her open again. She had circled back to the valley. And then her voice sounded farther and farther away until Jeb had to listen close to hear it.

A loud scream came from the far ridge and cold chills swept Jeb's body. He looked into the darkness, toward the far ridge. Then he heard the scream again. At first, Jeb had not been sure. But now he knew the sound. Only once before had he ever heard it. He had been with Jeptha, and Jeptha had told him never to forget it. This was the scream of a wildcat. This was the deadliest of all the game a hound could hunt here in the mountains. It was not often that a hound would stand against one and fight. And most of the hounds that did were either buried or left somewhere on the mountainside, never to be found.

Lucy bawled, and Jeb knew she was following a slow trail. And this was the mark of a good hound. There would be no hurry for Lucy. She would trail slowly, but always moving closer to her game. A fast hound would many times overrun the trail and have to drop back and pick it up again.

The wildcat screamed again and Jeb thought it was egging Lucy on. It was on the far ridge, the ridge that turned into Hurricane Hollow. Jeb thought it would wait until Lucy worked closer and then would turn down the ridge — not into the hollow where it would be trapped. The wildcat must know, Jeb thought, that Lucy was a slow trailer. There was a chance that a fast hound could turn the wildcat into the hollow and force it against the cliff. Against the cliff the wildcat would turn and fight.

Other than the loud scream that seemed to stop all the other sounds of the woods, Jeb was glad it was a wildcat. He loved to hear Lucy bark and he knew on the slow trail she would run all night. That is, if she were not called off. And he couldn't blow the horn.

He was glad in one way he couldn't blow the horn. He could stay on the mountaintop all night and he would be able to tell Grandma Quildy what had happened. Even Grandma Quildy knew that a hunter never left the mountain without his hound.

Jeb found himself a soft place to sit on and started to sit down. Then he jumped to his feet.

Along the far ridge drifted the bawl of another hound. At first Jeb thought it was the voice of Lucy, clear and deep. But the long bawls instead of the short, quick ones told him it wasn't. Other than this, the voice was the same. The dog was running, and Lucy would not bawl on the trail. Only when she had treed.

Deep and mellow the voice rang through the woods as though it were coming from a hollow log. It was hard to believe that another hound could have a voice so close to Lucy's. And then chills covered his body. He thought of the pup. There was a chance, Jeb knew, that the pup, being young on the trail, had heard the scream of the wildcat and had turned toward it, following sound instead of track.

Jeb caught his breath and listened to the steady bawl. He knew now it was the pup. And he was moving fast along the mountainside. So fast that he was sure to turn the wildcat into Hurricane Hollow. The wildcat screamed again, egging the young pup on, Jeb thought.

Once in the hollow the ground would be cleared

by the small creek that came out of it, and the pup
would move faster toward the cliff. Once against the
cliff, the wildcat would turn. The pup would not have
a chance. And yet, the pup had no way of knowing
the danger of the wildcat. He was only following the
sound.

From two hollows away came the voice of Lucy.
For the first time that Jeb could ever remember, Lucy
had lost the trail and had circled back to pick it up.
And into the hollow went the pup.

Jeb thought of the pup pushing the wildcat against
the rock cliff, and then being torn to pieces by its
sharp teeth and long claws. He thought of the pup
sticking his head into the air and bawling to let Jeb
know that he was a hound and was pushing his game.
And that he had no fear of the wildcat. With the blind
eye and stubtail he would face the wildcat, the deadliest of all the game here in the mountains.

Tears came to Jeb's eyes. And he called as loud as
he could.

"Mooneye!" he yelled. But his voice died in the
deep woods.

Jeb called again, and this time he started to run
through the trees toward the ridge. His only chance
was to try and catch the pup before it reached the cliff.
Jeb fell into the thick underbrush and got to his feet.

Tree limbs hit him in the face and brought more tears to his eyes. And the horn, swinging back and forth at his side, caught on low bushes and slowed him up. He pulled the horn from his shoulder and held it in his hand, crossing the ridge and into the hollow.

Jeb stopped to catch a short breath and listen. Behind him was the voice of Lucy, working the slow trail. By the time she reaches the cliff, Jeb thought, the pup will be killed.

Again and again the pup bawled, each time nearer the rock. In the hollow Jeb slipped on the slick stems of the wild fern and fell against the side of a large beech. The horn flew from his hand and into the air. Jed wiped his eyes and found the horn. He yelled again for the pup and headed for the cliff.

Close to the cliff Jeb stopped. Against the rock, its fur bristling, stood the wildcat. In front of the wildcat, his head low, stood the pup. He was not moving in, as Jeb had thought he would, but was baying the wildcat, staying at a safe distance but close enough to press the wildcat against the rock.

Jeb was afraid to call. If the pup knew he was this close, the sound of his voice might encourage it to move in on the wildcat. Jeb stood, tears streaming down his face, the horn hanging limp in his hand. Beneath the moon he could see the stubtail of the pup

moving back and forth. His head was turned to one side as if he was favoring the white eye. Then Jeb looked into the red eyes of the wildcat. He could hear the growl and see the sharp, white teeth. Lucy sounded again, closer, but not close enough. She was coming to the ridge, and for the first time Jeb was mad because she followed a slow trail. The wildcat crouched as if it was going to jump.

Jeb felt the horn. There was one way, he thought, to save the pup. He looked at the horn. One long blast and he knew Lucy would move over the ridge, coming to the sound. She was an old hound and had followed many trails. Once Jeb remembered Jeptha's saying that she was the only hound he would pit against a wildcat.

Jeb thought of the many days he had let the horn lie on the mantle while he had gone to the hillside garden. And he remembered why he had left the horn. But now, the white eye or stubtail of the pup no longer mattered. He knew he loved the small pup with all his might. The pup had found his trail and pushed his game like a true hound. It was Jeb who had failed. He knew that he could not blow the horn.

Tears welled in his eyes. Somewhere along the mountain, Jeb thought, Sampson once staggered. Maybe, Jeb thought, it was this same hollow. Sampson had found faith, enough faith to lift a whole mountain. Jeb looked again at the horn. It looked small compared to a mountain. He looked again toward the pup and the wildcat. Then he wiped his eyes and looked toward the moon.

"Lord," he said, "I know that that Book of Yours Grandma Quildy has is lots bigger than a box of doodlebugs. And I was ashamed of the pup You gave me, too. But I'm not ashamed any more. I haven't got the right to be a hunter, being that it takes a hunter to blow a horn. But if You are up there, Lord, like Grandma Quildy says, please let me blow it. I ain't got much time left and I got to call Lucy in."

Jeb raised the horn to his lips and took a deep breath. He blew with all his might. He blew until his face became red. And out of the end of the horn came nothing but wind. Trembling, Jeb pulled the horn from his lips.

"I ain't aiming to try and fool You this time, Lord," he said, and blew again.

The sweet music of the horn drifted through the deep woods and climbed the high ridge. And Jeb heard it echo over in the valley. And then the woods were quiet except for the whimper of the pup that had moved closer and the growl of the wildcat.

Through the brush came Lucy. She stopped in front

of Jeb wagging her long tail. Then she sniffed the air and jumped at the whimper of the pup. She turned and leaped onto the back of the wildcat.

Over and over they went, first Lucy on top and then the wildcat. Lucy was grabbing for its throat and the wildcat was trying to reach Lucy's stomach with its powerful claws. The pup jumped upon a ledge of the cliff and stood barking.

Lucy yelped and Jeb saw the red stream of blood come from her shoulder. The wildcat was on top now and Lucy fought to get up. Lucy yelped from the pain of the sharp claws.

The pup bawled into the air and with one long leap landed on the back of the wildcat. The pup rolled over and over on the ground, bouncing off the back of the wildcat. He had knocked the cat loose. The wildcat turned toward the pup. But before it could jump, Lucy had it by the throat. The pup ran around and around the wildcat, barking.

Finally Lucy let go of the wildcat and crawled away. And the wildcat lay still.

Jeb walked over and patted Lucy on the head. Her fur was covered with blood and Jeb wiped it with the sack he had tucked under his belt. Lucy licked his face as he lifted her in his arms and turned down the path that led out of the hollow. In front of him walked

the small pup, its head high in the air. It stopped once, looked back at Jeb and Lucy and walked on. Jeb watched the short tail moving back and forth.

The steep walls of the valley were so tall that Jeb could not see the top. The woods were dark with the tall trees of the mountain. Even the small saplings that sprouted in the hollow were taller than Jeb. The horn bounced against his side and he touched it with his hand. Jeb looked again toward the moon and he felt as big as Sampson.